THIS BOOK BELONGS TO

....

Copyright © 2015

make believe ideas ltd

The Wilderness, Berkhamsted, Hertfordshire, HP4 2AZ, UK.
501 Nelson Place, P.O. Box 141000, Nashville, TN 37214-1000, USA.

www.makebelieveideas.com

RAPUNZEL

Written by Helen Anderton

Illustrated by Stuart Lynch

make believe ideas

Reading together

This book is designed to be fun for children who are gaining confidence in their reading. They will enjoy and benefit from some time discussing the story with an adult. Here are some ways you can help your child take those first steps in reading:

❀ Encourage your child to look at the pictures and talk about what is happening in the story.

❀ Help your child to find familiar words and sound out the letters in harder words.

❀ Ask your child to read and repeat each short sentence.

Look at rhymes

Many of the sentences in this book are simple rhymes. Encourage your child to recognize rhyming words. Try asking the following questions:

❀ What does this word say?

❀ Can you find a word that rhymes with it?

❀ Look at the ending of two words that rhyme. Are they spelled the same? For example, "day" and "say," and "stare" and "hair."

Reading activities

The **What happens next?** activity encourages your child to retell the story and point to the mixed-up pictures in the right order.

The **Rhyming words** activity takes six words from the story and asks your child to read and find other words that rhyme with them.

The **Key words** pages provide practice with common words used in the context of the book. Read the sentences with your child and encourage him or her to make up more sentences using the key words listed around the border.

A **Picture dictionary** page asks children to focus closely on nine words from the story. Encourage your child to look carefully at each word, cover it with his or her hand, write it on a separate piece of paper, and finally, check it!

Do not complete all the activities at once – doing one each time you read will ensure that your child continues to enjoy the story and the time you are spending together. Have fun!

Gretel the witch simply hated her hair –
it was purple and so full of knots.
And what made it worse was living next door
to a girl who had long golden locks.

This girl, Rapunzel, had gold hair so long
that people would stop just to stare!
Gretel was jealous – she wanted a wig.
So she thought, "I'll steal that girl's hair!"

Hair!

Now, Gretel liked to grow spinach and beans,
which Rapunzel's mom hungrily spied.
"Steal us some beans!" she cried to her husband,
who willingly ran right outside.

Just at that moment, he heard a great POP –
the witch appeared out of the blue!
"My prize vegetables! You will pay for this!
I'll chop you up into a stew!"

Said the dad (turning pale), "Please spare my life!"
Grinning, the witch said, "I might . . .
Give me your daughter, and I'll let you go."
Shaking, the dad said, "All right!"

Gretel was thrilled that the wig of her dreams
would soon be in her power!
"I'll wait for her hair to grow longer," she thought,
and locked the girl in a tower.

With no tower door, Rapunzel would wait
until three o'clock every day.
That was the hour when Gretel arrived,
and cleared her throat loudly to say:

"Ahoy up there, let down your hair!"

Rapunzel threw down her very long plait
and Gretel climbed up in a flash.

She took out a ruler and measured the hair,
then said with a smile, "I must dash!"

One day, Rapunzel felt so alone
she started to sing a sad song.
As luck would have it, a charming young prince
heard her as he walked along.

He circled the tower – where was the door?
The walls were too high to climb!
But just at that moment, Gretel appeared
and shouted her usual rhyme:

"Ahoy up there, let down your hair!"

"So that's how it's done!" he thought to himself.
And the next day, to Rapunzel's surprise,

instead of the witch, the charming young prince appeared in front of her eyes!

The prince came to visit day after day
and everything was going fine,
'til one afternoon, when Gretel appeared
in the tower at just the same time!

Seeing the prince, she screamed out in rage,
   "Oi, you! Get away from that hair!"
She tried to push him out of the tower,
   but Rapunzel cried out, "Don't you dare!"

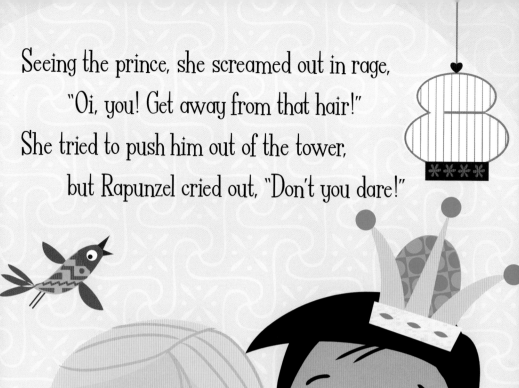

Quickly, Rapunzel cut off all her hair
and said (as glad as could be),

"Here, have my braid – I'll take the prince."
And with that, Rapunzel was free!

The pair were soon married (R. wore a hat).
And to show they had no hard feelings,
they invited the witch, who wore a wig
that was gold and reached to the ceiling!

What happens next?

Some of the pictures from the story have been mixed up! Can you retell the story and point to each picture in the correct order?

Rhyming words

Read the words in the middle of each group and point to the other words that rhyme with them.

air

dad

hair

hour

there

cat

flat

hat

gold

mom

climb

flower

tower

high

shower

braid

girl

curl

prince

twirl

big

wig

pig

push

song

ditch

witch

door

itch

knot

Now choose a word and make up a rhyming chant!

The **witch** had an **itch** in the **ditch**!

Key words

These sentences use common words to describe the story. Read the sentences and then make up new sentences for the other words in the border.

The witch **had** purple hair.

Rapunzel's hair **was** long.

Rapunzel's mom wanted **some** beans.

When the witch saw Rapunzel's dad, she was angry.

The witch **put** Rapunzel in a tower.

like · very · not

· big · put · with · day · an · can · we · are · up · had ·

The prince climbed **up** the tower.

The witch **saw** the prince.

Rapunzel cut **her** hair.

Rapunzel **and** the prince got married.

The witch wore a **big** wig.

the · a · and · to · saw · in · was · I · they · it · he · you · of · she · on · for · when

my · her · is · there · out · at · some · have · so · be ·

Picture dictionary

Look carefully at the pictures and the words.
Now cover the words, one at a time.
Can you remember how to write them?

climb

dad

plait

prince

ruler

spinach

tower

wig

witch